For Pete and Debbie at the Reading Reptile—
thanks for everything, especially Nate.—L. N.

For Whitney—my cute, charming,
and wonderful niece!—N. E.

Text copyright © 1998 by Laura Numeroff. Illustrations copyright © 1998 by Nate Evans.
All rights reserved under International and Pan-American Copyright Conventions.
Published in the United States by Random House, Inc., New York, and simultaneously
in Canada by Random House of Canada Limited, Toronto.

www.randomhouse.com/kids/

Library of Congress Cataloging-in-Publication Data

Numeroff, Laura.
Monster munchies / by Laura Numeroff ; illustrated by Nate Evans. p. cm.   "Beginner books."
SUMMARY: Hungry monsters eat everything in sight while introducing numbers one to twenty.
ISBN 0-679-89163-3 (trade). — ISBN 0-679-99163-8 (lib. bdg.)
[1. Monsters—Fiction. 2. Counting. 3. Stories in rhyme.] I. Evans, Nate, ill. II. Title.
PZ8.3.N92Mo 1998 [E]—dc21 97-48559

Printed in the United States of America 10 9 8 7 6 5 4 3 2 1

Monster Munchies

★ BY LAURA NUMEROFF ★

. illustrated by Nate Evans .

BEGINNER BOOKS

A Division of Random House, Inc.

One giant monster
wears a dress,
eats the couch,
and makes a mess.

Two happy monsters
clean the room.
When they're done,
they eat the broom.

Three yellow monsters
at my door
come inside
and eat the floor.

Four tiny monsters
on the bus.
Hear them burp
and make a fuss.

Five grouchy monsters
go to school,

eat their desks,
and think they're cool.

Six purple monsters

down the hall

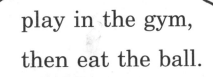

play in the gym,
then eat the ball.

Seven silly monsters
in a car
eat the wheels.
They won't get far!

Eight bumpy monsters,
red as beets,
stop to talk
and eat the seats.

Nine fuzzy monsters
make a cake,

then eat the bowl

before they bake.

Ten baby monsters
hear a noise,
get upset,
then eat their toys.

Eleven blue monsters
in a band
eat the music
on their stand.

Twelve tall monsters
at the dance
drink some punch
and eat their pants.

Thirteen striped monsters
counting sheep
eat their bed
and get no sleep.

Fourteen green monsters,
way up high,
gobble clouds
as they zoom by.

Fifteen old monsters
fly a kite,
eat the string,
then start to fight.

Sixteen fat monsters
with their pails
eat some sand,
then ride on whales.

Seventeen pink monsters
build a barn,
eat the roof,
then knit with yarn.

Eighteen scared monsters
feed the pigs,
eat the fence,
then put on wigs.

Nineteen thin monsters
wave good-bye,
eat their hats,
then start to cry.

Twenty hungry monsters
with nothing left to chew.
Better close this book up tight...

Before they chew on **you!**